The Little Matcl

MORMON TABERNACLE CHOIR CONCERT SERIES

The Little Match Girl

HANS CHRISTIAN ANDERSEN'S CLASSIC TALE

RETOLD BY

David Warner

PAINTINGS BY

Greg Newbold

SHADOW
MOUNTAIN

MORMON
TABERNACLE
CHOIR

Mormon Tabernacle Choir is an ambassador for The Church of Jesus Christ of Latter-day Saints.

Text © 2017 Intellectual Reserve, Inc. All rights reserved.

Illustrations © 2017 Gregory L. Newbold

Art direction by Richard Erickson

Design by Sheryl Dickert Smith

Visit us at ShadowMountain.com

Library of Congress Cataloging-in-Publication Data

Names: Warner, David T. (David Terry), 1963– author. | Newbold, Greg, illustrator. | Andersen, H. C. (Hans Christian), 1805–1875. Lille pige med svovlstikkerne.

Title: The little match girl / retold by David Warner ; illustrated by Greg Newbold.

Description: Salt Lake City, Utah : Shadow Mountain, [2017] | The classic children's story The Little Match Girl, by Hans Christian Andersen, is retold for a Christmas audience as part of the annual Christmas concert series hosted by the Mormon Tabernacle Choir. | Summary: The wares of the little match girl illuminate her cold world, bringing some beauty to her brief, tragic life.

Identifiers: LCCN 2017017817 | ISBN 9781629723594 (hardbound : alk. paper)

Subjects: | CYAC: Fairy tales.

Classification: LCC PZ8.W217 Li 2017 | DDC [E]—dc23

LC record available at https://lccn.loc.gov/2017017817

Printed in the United States of America   8/2017

Publishers Printing, Salt Lake City, Utah

10   9   8   7   6   5   4   3   2   1

Hans Christian Andersen's *The Little Match Girl*

Few storytellers have woven more timeless and beloved tales than Danish author Hans Christian Andersen. From his fairy tales to his poetry to his plays, Andersen captured the depths of the human experience and crafted stories that have resonated through the ages.

Born in 1805 in humble circumstances, Andersen developed a love of literature and the dramatic at an early age. In his youth, he wrote his own versions of fairy tales he had learned in childhood. In time, he was fabricating his own fantastical stories, sparking the imaginations of readers for generations to come.

But Andersen was also a keen observer of human nature, recognizing that life's most beautiful lessons often come as a result of some sorrow. Such is the case in his 1845 short story "The Little Match Girl." Though on the surface, the little girl seems the picture of misery and despair, her story is one of hope for a better life and assurance that a joyous reunion in heaven is awaiting even God's most helpless children. Despite her suffering, the little girl finds warmth and light, ever believing that all will be right in the end. It is a message that has stood the test of time—and one that reminds each of us to look for ways to bring the warmth of love and light of understanding to others.

It was nearly nightfall. The orphan girl blinked away thick snowflakes falling in her eyes. Everyone in the great city was bundled and busy, heads down, eyes fixed on the black cobblestones peeking up through packed snow. A wagon spewed freezing slush across the girl's loosely wrapped feet. "Out of the way," its heavy wheels grumbled. But the shivering child was not afraid and did not step back. She stood bravely, silently, holding out all she had in the world—her last bundle of wooden matches, saved for selling this Christmas Eve.

As the tide of darkness rose in side streets and alleyways, the throngs ebbed across courtyards, around corners, and down dimly lit passageways. Pushed along by the frosty wind, they hurried home for their Christmas giving, passing the little match girl, unaware.

When finally only stray dogs crisscrossed the empty streets, the frail girl retreated to a corner between two stone houses. Sliding down against the cold wall, she tucked her matches in her pocket and her hands under her arms, lifted her knees, and warmed her face in the shreds of a threadbare apron. But she couldn't look down for long. The Christmas stars above were calling her to look up and out. As she did, she spied the yellow light of a gas lamp, burning atop its cast-iron post. It was a small but steady flame, like the faith that flickered in her heart. If only she could climb up and warm herself in its glow.

But wait, she thought, digging into her apron pocket. *I already have a fire of my own!* Drawing a single match from the bundle, she rubbed the tip along the stone wall. *Whischt!* In an instant, the match was blazing before her. As she held her hand in front of the flame, she found herself basking in the glow of a radiant stove. Nearby, a kindly woman was filling the kindling basket, to keep the fire burning. And for the first time, the little match girl felt she was not alone.

The child stretched out her feet. "Ahhh! At last!" she smiled. Firelight kissed her delicate fingers and toes, and she wiggled them with delight. The air itself enfolded her in a soft blanket of kindness.

But as her eyes closed in relief, the match blew out and the fire disappeared. "No! No! Come back!" she cried. Plunging her hands into her apron, she seized another match. *Just one more*, she thought, hoping to make the friendly hearth reappear.

Whischt! Again, a long golden flame reached up before the child. As she studied its graceful curl, bright lights flickered in her shining eyes. She imagined she was staring into the glow of a magnificent chandelier. Suddenly, the wall of the stone house became transparent, like a veil, and she could see a stately dining room within. Fir garlands, parchment decorations, and Christmas candles adorned the elegant hall. The same gentle woman was laying the table—a soft white cloth, a porcelain platter, a roast goose, and sweet bread brimming with spices and candied fruit. For a moment, the child's lips parted with wonder.

But again, as the little girl closed her eyes to breathe in the savory aroma, a snowflake landed on the match, and a wisp of smoke rose into the night air and vanished. "Come back, come back," she whispered.

Frantically, she reached for another match. Before she could stop herself, she was striking it against the wall. *Whischt!* In the flash of light, she saw a sparkling silver ornament. It was held by a woman's graceful hands and carefully placed on the green boughs of a towering Christmas tree. Slowly the child lifted her eyes—up, up, up. A thousand candle lights. A hundred thousand facets of beauty and wonder and joy. Stars dancing in the sky. *Yes*, she thought, *this is heaven.*

Even as the child gasped with delight, her eyes closed and the match went out. The brilliant stars tumbled down, and in their shimmering tails the great tree disappeared.

Bowing her head, she pushed her frozen chin into her chest, where warm tears pooled. Some drops fell onto her freezing hands, and instinctively she covered the last of her matches. A fire in the stove, a feast on the table, candles on the tree. *How could these be gone?* she wondered. There was something real in them. Something alive. Something waiting.

Believing as only a child can, she lifted the remaining bundle of matches and spoke to them simply: "Can you bring Christmas back? Can you give me that beautiful world again?" With a prayer pounding in her heart, she boldly scraped the cluster of tips against the wall—all of them at once. *Whischt!* For a moment, nothing came. But then, slowly, a single flame took hold and burst into a bouquet of fire.

As the little match girl peered into the blaze, she heard a voice she remembered from long ago. "Come, little one." She knew this rustling of skirts, this soft, sweet fragrance.

"Grandmother," she whispered, turning around. "You're here!"

With a tender sigh, the woman sank to her knees. "As I have always been."

Then, like a great swan spreading her wings, the woman wrapped her granddaughter in a shawl of pure white wool. The shreds of the child's gray dress miraculously became a gossamer white gown. Grandmother took her tiny hand, now beautifully pink and perfectly clean, and drew her close. "I have come to you, my child, so you can come with me."

As they rose silently into the night, the child felt warmth flow into her feet and legs. Her dress was full now, with petticoats flowing and a pretty blue sash dancing in the winter wind. She looked out. The new white snow sparkled across rooftops as far as she could see, and moonlight transformed the river into a silvery satin ribbon.

For just a moment the little match girl looked down into the corner between the two stone houses. Alas, a waif was resting quietly against the wall, burned-out matchsticks scattered around her, a smile of perfect contentment on her lips.

When I come back, I will bring that brave child more Christmas matches, she thought to herself. *I'll bring a whole bundle of them!*

Squeezing her grandmother's hand, she looked up into the warm, lustrous light. Stars were gathering in the open portals, waiting to dance with her for joy. She would never look down again.

The next morning, people passing by glanced at the child's body and turned their eyes away. They could only imagine she had been abandoned there, alone in the darkness. But the truth is, she was never alone. She had drawn on the light she had—on everything within her—to kindle the visions of Christmas. And in return, Christmas had brought her the love of family, the mercy of heaven, and a pathway home. As thick snowflakes fell in the little match girl's eyes, her tears were washed away. And the fire in her heart burned on, bright and strong, forever.

On This Holy Night

From "The Little Match Girl"

"The Little Match Girl" was first presented in the annual Christmas concert of the Mormon Tabernacle Choir and Orchestra at Temple Square, read by Rolando Villazón. During the reading, a version of this Christmas hymn was sung by the Choir, with music by Mack Wilberg and text by David Warner.

On this holy night,
Once host to heaven's joy,
All heaven gathered 'round
To welcome heaven's boy.
May we this Christmas eve,
As angels at His birth,
Enfold His little ones
In love and peace on earth.

In the winter's chill
His spark becomes a flame
When Christmas gifts of love
Bespeak His blessed name.
*For He's the **Christmas fire***
That melts the fearful soul,
And heals the wounded heart,
And makes our spirits whole.

When the cupboard's bare
*And we've no **Christmas feast**,*
Humility is born,
And love for all, increased.

Then, how our cup o'erflows;
Our table, He prepares,
And wondrously, we dine
With angels, unawares!

If, when the leaves are flown,
All nature seems to sleep,
*A **Christmas tree** assures*
His promise He will keep.
So, cheerfully behold
The bright tree of His grace,
Partake of His sweet love,
And see His smiling face.

On this holy night,
The world in darkness lay,
Yet earth rolls on her wings,
God's glory to display.
May we, this Christmas eve,
Press even through the night,
To love His children, all,
And lead them to His light.

Every December, one of the many wonders of Christmas in Salt Lake City is the annual concert of the Mormon Tabernacle Choir and Orchestra at Temple Square, a Temple Square tradition for decades. Since the turn of the twenty-first century, these popular concerts have delighted live audiences of over 60,000 people each year in the LDS Conference Center, with millions more tuning in each year to *Christmas with the Mormon Tabernacle Choir* on PBS television. It is a full-scale production featuring world-class musicians, soloists, dancers, narrators, and music that delights and inspires viewers year after year.

Each concert has featured a special guest artist, including internationally acclaimed tenor Rolando Villazón (2016); the beloved Muppets® from Sesame Street® (2014); Broadway actors and singers Laura Osnes (2015), Santino Fontana (2014), Alfie Boe (2012), and Brian Stokes Mitchell (2011); famous baritones Bryn Terfel (2003) and Nathan Gunn (2011); opera divas Deborah Voigt (2013), Renée Fleming (2005), and Frederica von Stade (2003); *American Idol* finalist David Archuleta (2010); and multiple Grammy Award–winner Natalie Cole (2009). The remarkable talents of award-winning actors Jane Seymour (2011) and Edward Herrmann (2008), plus British actors Martin Jarvis (2015), John Rhys-Davies (2013), and Michael York (2010) have graced the stage, sharing memorable stories of the season. The esteemed list of featured narrators also includes famed broadcast journalist Tom Brokaw (2012), two-time Pulitzer Prize–winning author David McCullough (2009), and noted TV news anchorman Walter Cronkite (2002).

The 360 members of the Mormon Tabernacle Choir represent men and women from many different backgrounds and professions and range in age from twenty-five to sixty. Their companion ensemble, the Orchestra at Temple Square, includes over 150 musicians who accompany the Choir on broadcasts, recordings, and tours. All serve as unpaid volunteers, reflecting a rich tapestry of unique lives and experiences, brought together by their love of performing and their faith in God.

The Mormon Tabernacle Choir has appeared at thirteen world's fairs and expositions, performed at the inaugurations of seven US presidents, and sung for numerous worldwide telecasts and special events. Five of the Mormon Tabernacle Choir's recordings have achieved "gold record" and two have achieved "platinum record" status. Its recordings have reached the #1 position on *Billboard*® magazine's classical lists a remarkable twelve times since 2003.

This story of "The Little Match Girl" was originally written for the 2016 Christmas concert, narrated by Rolando Villazón with music by the Choir and Orchestra. You can enjoy that performance, which includes a version of the Christmas hymn on the previous page, at www.motab.org/littlematchgirl.